My Secret Unicorn

Moonlight Journey

Linda Chapman

Illustrated by Ann Kronheimer

PUFFIN

Penguin ... 4, USA
Pengui ... ntario,

Penguin ... Australia

Penguin Books India Pvt Ltd, 11 Community Centre, Panchsheel Park, New Delhi – 110 017, India
Penguin Group (NZ), 67 Apollo Drive, Mairangi Bay, Auckland 1310, New Zealand (a division of Pearson New Zealand Ltd)
Penguin Books (South Africa) (Pty) Ltd, 24 Sturdee Avenue, Rosebank, Johannesburg 2196, South Africa

Penguin Books Ltd, Registered Offices: 80 Strand, London WC2R 0RL, England

penguin.com

Published 2007
008

Typeset in Bembo by Palimpsest Book Production Limited, Grangemouth, Stirlingshire

Made and printed in England by Clays Ltd, St Ives plc

British Library Cataloguing in Publication Data
A CIP catalogue record for this book is available from the British Library

ISBN: 978–0–141–32121–9

www.greenpenguin.co.uk

Penguin Books is committed to a sustainable future for our business, our readers and our planet. This book is made from Forest Stewardship Council™ certified paper.

a hug for goo…
back and fished the map out of h…
'There's a big craggy mountain that we h…
to head towards. I think we'll see it once
we've flown over the woods. Fly as fast as
you can!'

Bo

THE MAGIC

DREAMS COME TR

FLYING HIGH

STARLIGHT SURPRISE

STRONGER THAN MAGIC

A SPECIAL FRIEND

A WINTER WISH

A TOUCH OF MAGIC

SNOWY DREAMS

TWILIGHT MAGIC

FRIENDS FOREVER

RISING STAR

MOONLIGHT JOURNEY

Special thanks to Gill Harvey

CHAPTER One

The afternoon sun glinted through the trees as Lauren watched her friend Mel ride Shadow towards the gnarled trunk. An old hickory tree had fallen halfway across the woodland path, and it was perfect for jumping over. 'Come on, Shadow, you can do it!' Lauren whispered.

The dapple-grey pony took one long

stride, then one short one. He sized up the trunk, tucked up his front feet, and sailed over it.

'Well done, Shadow!' cried Lauren. 'That was brilliant!'

Her pony, Twilight, snorted, as though he was agreeing with her. Lauren smiled. She knew he understood every word she said. Twilight might look like a little grey pony, but he was much, much more than that. When Lauren said the secret words of the Turning Spell, Twilight turned into a beautiful unicorn, with a snow-white coat and a shimmering horn. Since she had first made this amazing discovery, Lauren and Twilight had been gradually finding out about his magical powers. One of them was that he could use his horn to give courage and confidence, and he had once helped his friend Shadow to become confident about jumping.

Mel was trotting back to Lauren, her cheeks flushed with excitement. 'Aren't you going to have a go?' she called.

Lauren grinned. 'You try stopping us!' She gathered up her reins and nudged Twilight into a trot, then turned him towards the log and asked him to canter. Twilight surged forward, but steadied as he approached the log. He eyed it up carefully before bounding easily over the tree trunk.

'Brilliant!' cried Mel.

Lauren bent forward and patted Twilight as he arched his neck and proudly tossed his mane. She knew he was enjoying himself. Twilight couldn't speak to Lauren while he was a pony, but she was pretty good at telling what he was feeling anyway. She slowed him back to a trot, then turned and rode back towards Mel. 'That was fantastic,' she said. 'Shall we carry on to the clearing? We can do more jumping there.'

Lauren smiled to herself. She wished she could tell Mel exactly why Shadow loved jumping now, but one of the most important things about being a Unicorn Friend was keeping all the unicorn magic a secret. She often wondered what her best friends, Mel and Jess, would think if she told them that Twilight was really a unicorn!

Together, the girls turned their ponies

down the track and trotted deeper into the woods, where the spring buds were just appearing on the trees. The clearing was one of their favourite places. There were banks to ride up and down, and fallen logs and brushwood that were great for jumping over. It was like having their very own mini cross-country course.

When they arrived, Lauren took a moment to decide which route to take with Twilight. He was used to all but the biggest logs by now, so she chose a course that would be lots of fun, with plenty of twists and turns. Sure enough, he tackled them all with his ears pricked up, springing over every jump with miles to spare. He even bucked playfully when he'd finished, and Lauren laughed out loud.

Mel and Shadow followed, taking a different route that avoided a couple of the more tricky jumps. But Shadow seemed as happy as Twilight to be jumping, his tail flying high as he cleared the final pile of brushwood.

'That was great!' Mel laughed. 'Let's do it again!'

Lauren pushed Twilight back into a canter. This time she decided to try riding down one of the steepest banks. Twilight tucked his hocks underneath him, then slid forward for a little way before jumping down safely.

'Well done, Twilight!' Lauren praised him. They cantered around the rest of the jumps, then watched as Mel and Shadow took yet another route, weaving a figure of eight around the course. Shadow cleared everything before trotting back to Lauren and Twilight. He stood there, panting and tossing his head.

'Maybe we should stop now,' Mel said. 'Shadow seems all puffed out.' She patted his neck. 'He's quite sweaty too. He must be a bit unfit – Twilight looks absolutely fine!'

Lauren stroked Twilight's neck. His coat felt perfectly dry. She wondered if Twilight was fitter than Shadow because he got exercise at night as well, when he did lots of flying around as a unicorn. But she couldn't tell Mel that. 'Maybe we should spend more time doing trotting exercises instead of always hacking in the woods,' she suggested. 'That's good for keeping ponies fit.'

'Good idea,' said Mel, as they turned

the ponies on to the homeward track. 'It's tempting to come to the woods every day, but I want Shadow to be as fit as he can be so we can keep on jumping!'

After supper that night, Lauren went upstairs to her bedroom to do her homework. It was Friday night, so she had all weekend to do it – but she decided it would be much better to get it out of the way quickly. She had to write a paragraph about her favourite hobby, so she described herself and Twilight jumping with Mel and Shadow in the woods. Writing about something like that felt more like fun than homework! When she finished, she had just enough time to visit Twilight before bed.

Lauren pulled on a thick sweater and stepped on to the landing. Her younger brother, Max, was already in bed. His Bernese mountain dog, Buddy, lay stretched outside Max's bedroom door with his head on his paws. He looked up at Lauren and thumped his tail on the carpet as she passed. She smiled and patted his head. Before slipping downstairs Lauren noticed that there was a light shining from under the study door. Lauren's mum wrote children's books for a living, and Lauren remembered that she had a deadline to meet. She could be busy for hours yet!

Lauren popped her head round the living-room door, where her dad was watching the news on TV. 'I'm just going out to see Twilight, Dad,' she said.

'OK, Lauren,' replied her dad. 'Don't be too long.'

'I won't be,' Lauren promised, shrugging on her jacket and heading outside into the cool spring evening. This was the moment she looked forward to every night – the moment she turned Twilight into a unicorn. Twilight was waiting for her at the paddock gate, and whinnied when he saw her.

Lauren wrapped her arms around his

neck, then led him across the paddock out of sight of the house. Once they were safely hidden by some trees, she stroked his nose, and whispered the words of the Turning Spell.

'Twilight Star, Twilight Star,
Twinkling high above so far.
Shining light, shining bright,
Will you grant my wish tonight?
Let my little horse forlorn
Be at last a unicorn!'

There was a flash of purple light, then Twilight the little grey pony was gone; instead, a dazzling unicorn with a silky white mane and tail stood next to her.

Twilight nudged Lauren's arm. 'Are we going flying tonight?' he asked. When he spoke, his mouth didn't move, but Lauren could hear his voice in her head as long as she kept a hair from his mane in her pocket.

Lauren smiled. 'Of course we are, but we will have to be quick. Dad said not to be long.' Then she remembered how tired Shadow had been that afternoon. 'If you don't feel too tired, that is,' she added. 'You and Shadow did lots of jumping earlier!'

'Oh, I feel fine,' said Twilight. 'But I'm a bit worried about Shadow. When we were walking back through the woods, he told me he wasn't feeling very well.'

'Poor Shadow,' said Lauren. 'So he wasn't puffing because he's unfit, after all. Maybe he's getting a cold.'

Twilight shook his head. 'He said he's had colds before, but this was different. He didn't understand it – he said he was just feeling tired out and a bit strange.'

The unicorn rested his muzzle on Lauren's arm, and his eyes looked sad. Lauren could see that Twilight was worried about his pony friend.

'Let's go and see him,' she suggested. 'Maybe he'll be feeling better now that he's had a chance to rest.'

Twilight nodded his head. 'That's a good idea,' he agreed.

Lauren swung herself on to Twilight's back. She buried her hands in his mane and touched her heels to his sides. 'Come on, let's go!'

CHAPTER TWO

Twilight soared into the air, his silky mane shimmering in the moonlight. Lauren gazed down at her house. Its windows became tiny yellow boxes of light as Twilight flew upward, then they disappeared altogether as he turned towards Goose Creek Farm, where Mel lived. Lauren felt the wind tugging at her hair, and she hugged

Twilight's neck happily. There was nothing better than flying – nothing in the whole world!

Lauren loved being a Unicorn Friend but she knew that there was more to it than flying through the night with Twilight. Unicorns were supposed to use their magic to help people and animals in trouble. Lauren and Twilight had solved lots of problems since they had discovered Twilight's magical powers, but they had also learned only to use his magic for important things.

Twilight began to descend towards the farmhouse, but circled around slowly before going too close. Lauren peered over his shoulder, scanning the yard below for any sign of people. To her relief, the lights in the tack room and the feed room were off – so everyone had gone indoors for the night.

'I think it's safe to go down,' she said. It was very important that no one else saw Twilight in his unicorn form.

Twilight landed lightly by Shadow's stable and Lauren slipped off his back. She listened for a moment to check that there really was no one around. Then she slid back the bolt on the half-door, and Twilight followed her inside.

Shadow was lying down in the straw. 'Hello, Shadow,' Lauren whispered, crouching down beside him. 'We've come to see how you're feeling.'

Twilight bent his head down to nuzzle the dapple-grey pony, and he whickered a greeting. But Shadow didn't even try to get up. He just raised his head a little, then let it flop back down again.

Lauren watched anxiously as the two ponies spoke to each other in their own special language. 'Is he feeling any better?' she asked Twilight.

'He says he feels worse than he did earlier today, and he can't breathe properly,' Twilight said worriedly.

Lauren frowned. It sounded as though Shadow might be really ill. They had to do something to help him. 'Perhaps you should use your magic to make him better,' she suggested.

Twilight blinked his big brown eyes, and nodded. 'Yes,' he agreed. 'I think I should try.' Being able to heal things was one of his magical powers. He reached down and touched Shadow's neck with his horn, which seemed to glow a little brighter.

Lauren held her breath and waited for Shadow to get to his feet. When Twilight's horn glowed, it usually meant the magic was working. But Shadow just groaned and closed his eyes, then stretched his neck out on the straw. Twilight was very worried, and Lauren was puzzled. 'Maybe your magic doesn't always work straight away,' she said.

Twilight twitched one ear doubtfully. 'Maybe.'

They waited for a few more minutes, but Shadow still didn't seem any better. His eyes stayed closed, and it looked as if he was trying to go to sleep.

Lauren stroked Shadow's cheek, then stood up. 'We'd better not stay any longer,' she said. 'But we'll come back and see you tomorrow, Shadow. I'm sure you'll be fine by then.'

She waited for Twilight to say goodbye to the sick pony. Then, as quietly as they could, she and Twilight left the stable.

'I hope Shadow gets better quickly. He's my best pony friend,' said Twilight as they flew over the woods towards home.

They landed by his stable. Lauren slipped down off his back and gave him a hug. 'Of course he will,' she said.

She whispered the words that changed

Twilight back into a shaggy grey pony. 'Goodnight, Twilight,' she said. 'I'm sure your magic will have worked by the morning.'

But Twilight hung his head, and Lauren knew he wouldn't be happy until he was sure that Shadow was better. With a heavy heart, she kissed his soft nose and headed inside. Her mum was still working in her study, and her dad was on the phone. Lauren said goodnight and went upstairs to bed.

Lauren tossed and turned under her duvet, worrying about Shadow. She wondered if Mel knew he was ill. Maybe she should have let her friend know before they left Goose Creek Farm tonight. But how? Mel would have been astonished if Lauren had turned up on her doorstep so late at night! And now Twilight was miserable too. Eventually she drifted off, but she woke early and couldn't get back to sleep again. With a sigh, she rubbed her eyes and got up. She pulled on her jeans and a sweatshirt and plodded down to the kitchen for breakfast.

'What are you up to today?' asked her mother.

'I'm going to ride over to see Mel and Shadow,' said Lauren as she slowly poured out some cereal into her bowl.

'OK,' said Mrs Foster, stifling a yawn.

'Max has taken Buddy to visit Steve and Leo, so I'm glad you have something to do too. I'm sorry I'm so busy, sweetheart. I stayed up late working on my manuscript, but I still haven't finished. I'm going to be busy for most of the day.'

'That's fine, Mum,' Lauren said. Her mum's job meant that she sometimes worked very odd hours but she was always at home, so Lauren and Max could call her if they needed her. 'You know I love going over to see Mel on Twilight.'

Mrs Foster smiled. 'Have fun then,' she said.

'I will.' Lauren swallowed a few

spoonfuls of cereal and headed for the door. 'See you later.'

As usual, Twilight was standing by the paddock gate. Lauren's heart lifted at the sight of the little grey pony waiting for her, and she tried to push away her worries from the night before. She gave him a hug, then fetched his breakfast of carrots, apples and pony nuts. While Twilight munched his way through the bucket, she went to get his saddle and bridle.

'We'll go straight over to see Mel and Shadow,' she said, sliding the saddle on to his back. 'I'm sure Shadow will be feeling a lot better.'

Twilight snorted, and nuzzled her

elbow. Lauren guessed he was saying that he hoped so too.

It wasn't far to Goose Creek Farm, and they were soon trotting up the driveway. Normally Mel would run out to greet them, but there was no sign of her today. As Twilight trotted into the yard, Mel's face appeared over Shadow's door.

'Oh, Lauren!' she burst out the minute she saw them. 'I'm so glad you've come. I think Shadow must be really ill!'

Lauren's heart sank. Twilight's magic hadn't worked after all. She climbed down from the saddle and led Twilight to the door, then peered in. Shadow was lying in the straw, breathing heavily. He didn't look up, not even when Twilight whinnied to him. If anything, he looked even worse than he had last night.

'Poor Shadow,' Lauren murmured. She tied Twilight to the ring outside Shadow's stable so that he could look over the half-door, then opened the door quietly and let herself in.

'My mum's just gone to call the vet,' said Mel. She was kneeling down by Shadow's head, stroking his cheek. Her voice wobbled a little bit, and Lauren noticed that she was trying to blink away tears. 'He's never been like this before, not even when he's had a cold.'

Lauren knelt down next to her and put an arm around her friend. 'I'm sure he'll be fine,' she said reassuringly.

'I hope so,' said Mel, biting her lip. 'I hope the vet gets here soon.'

Lauren wasn't sure what else to say. Why hadn't Twilight's unicorn magic worked? She glanced up at Twilight, feeling anxious. Twilight was standing very still, hanging his head as he gazed down at his friend. She guessed he was thinking the same thing.

'We'll wait with you,' she told Mel. 'We won't leave you here on your own.'

Mel gave a little smile. 'Thank you,' she said.

At last Mr Blackstone, the local vet, arrived and came over to the stable with Mel's mum. He examined Shadow thoroughly, listening carefully to the pony's heart and his breathing.

'Has he been off his food?' he asked Mel.

'Yes. He ate hardly any of his haynet last night,' Mel told him.

Mr Blackstone looked at the colour of the skin around Shadow's eyes, then checked inside his mouth.

'Well, he's definitely feeling quite poorly,' he said. 'But it's hard to tell what's wrong with him. It's not colic, or anything like that. It's probably a virus. I'll have to take a blood test to find out.'

'Will it hurt?' Mel asked, as Mr Blackstone took a syringe out of his bag.

'No, no. It's just a little pinprick,' he assured her. Mel and Lauren held their breath while he concentrated on inserting the syringe. 'There we are. All done.'

'So . . . will he get better?' asked Mel, in a small voice.

'Oh, I'm sure he will,' said Mr Blackstone. He packed the syringe into his bag, and stood up. 'I'll let you know as soon as the results come in. Hopefully that will give me an idea of how I can treat him. Keep him warm and comfortable, and don't disturb him too much. If it's a virus, he'll need plenty of rest.' Then he smiled. 'Try not to worry. I'm sure everything will be fine.'

'Thank you,' Mel said bravely. 'I'll try.'

As they watched Mel's mother walk

the vet back to his car, Lauren squeezed Mel's arm. She knew how her friend must be feeling. Twilight had only been ill once, when he and Lauren had been using his magic for things that weren't important. Lauren had been very, very anxious.

'I'll fetch Shadow's rug,' said Mel. 'That will keep him nice and warm.'

The girls went to the tack room for Shadow's rug, then went back to his stall. They couldn't put it on properly with him lying down, so they just laid it over him and tucked it in at the edges.

Mel sat down on the straw by Shadow's head. Her face was clouded with worry, and Lauren wasn't sure how to comfort her. She wished she could discuss everything with Twilight, but she wouldn't be able to talk to him properly until later that evening.

After a while, Mel's mum appeared at the door. 'Why don't you two come inside?' she suggested. 'I'll be making some lunch soon. Mr Blackstone said that Shadow needs to rest. We can put Twilight in the stable next to Shadow's.'

Mel looked doubtful. 'I don't want to leave Shadow on his own,' she said.

Just then Shadow stirred restlessly, and closed his eyes. 'He needs to sleep,' said Mel's mum. 'He might find that easier if you're not here.'

'I suppose you're right. We should just

let him lie quietly.' Mel stroked Shadow's ears, then bent down and kissed his muzzle. 'We'll be back later, Shadow,' she promised.

Lauren led Twilight into the other stable. She took off his saddle and bridle and gave him a haynet to eat. Kissing his nose, she let herself out of the stable. Mel followed her across the yard, her footsteps slow and dragging. Inside the farmhouse, Lauren suggested that they both play on Mel's game console while her mum got lunch ready. She hoped it might take Mel's mind off Shadow out in the yard. But Lauren could tell that Mel's heart wasn't in the game because Lauren kept on winning, which was very unusual. Mel normally beat her without even trying.

Then Mel's mum tried to cheer her up with her favourite lunch – fish fingers and home-made chips. But that didn't work either. Mel just played with the food on her plate and left most of her chips.

After lunch, they looked through Mel's old pony magazines and cut out their favourite pictures to stick in a scrapbook. But Mel kept stopping whenever she found a picture of a dapple-grey pony like Shadow, and Lauren could tell she was trying not to cry. The clock at the bottom of the stairs chimed four, and Lauren realized it was time to go.

'I told my mum I'd be back before dinner,' she said. 'I'm sorry I can't stay longer, Mel.'

'That's OK,' Mel said. 'Thanks for coming, Lauren. It's really helped.'

But she still didn't look very happy.

The two girls headed back out to the yard, and looked over the stable door. To Lauren's dismay, Shadow hadn't moved. In fact, his sides seemed to be heaving up and down more than ever.

Mel's face was pale. 'His breathing sounds worse,' she said, her voice barely above a whisper. As Lauren led Twilight out of his stall, she saw one lonely tear roll down her friend's face.

Mel scrubbed at her face with the back of her hand. 'I don't know what I'll do if something happens to Shadow,' she said.

Lauren gave her friend a hug. 'I know exactly what you mean,' she said, desperately wanting to comfort her. 'We just have to hope that he gets better. I'm sure he will. That's what the vet said, wasn't it?'

Mel gave a watery smile. 'Yes. Thanks, Lauren.'

But as Lauren rode away, she wished that Mel had something better to thank her for. Somehow, she and Twilight *had* to find a way to help Shadow.

CHAPTER Three

When Lauren reached home, her mum was singing in the kitchen as she scrubbed potatoes. Lauren knew that meant she'd finished her manuscript.

'Hi, Lauren,' said Mrs Foster, waving the potato brush at her. 'Have you had a nice day?'

Lauren shook her head. 'Shadow's really sick,' she said. 'And the vet doesn't know what's wrong. He had to do a blood test to find out what it is.'

'Oh dear,' said Mrs Foster, her smile fading. 'Is Twilight OK? You don't think he's caught it too, do you?'

'No, he's fine,' said Lauren. For a moment, she wished more than anything that she could tell her mum how upset Twilight was feeling about his friend, and about the fact that his powers couldn't heal Shadow. But she stopped herself just in time.

'Well, I'm sure Shadow will get better once they've found out what the problem is,' said Mrs Foster, pricking the potatoes with a fork. 'Try not to fret too much, honey.'

She put the potatoes into the oven. 'Maybe you need to take your mind off it. Do you want to come into town with me while the potatoes are baking? Your dad can keep an eye on them. I have to collect some dry-cleaning. We'll pick up Max and Buddy on the way back.'

Lauren instantly had a spark of an idea. A trip into town meant that she could go to the bookshop and speak to Mrs Fontana. She was the only other person who knew that Twilight was a unicorn. In fact, it was Mrs Fontana who had helped Lauren to discover his wonderful secret. She knew so much about ponies and unicorns – maybe she would know what to do to help Shadow! 'Oh yes, that would be great,' she said. 'Can I go to the bookshop?'

'Of course you can,' said Mrs Foster. 'But it will have to be a short visit this time.'

Lauren ran upstairs to change. Before dashing downstairs again, she looked out of her bedroom window to check on Twilight. He was standing by the fence with his head hanging low, looking gloomy.

'We'll find a way to help Shadow,' Lauren whispered. 'Mrs Fontana will have some ideas, I'm sure she will.' Then she bounded down the stairs and out to the car, where her mum was waiting.

Ten minutes later, Mrs Foster pulled up outside the bookshop. 'See you soon,' she called, as Lauren clambered out.

'OK. Thanks, Mum,' said Lauren, and she hurried inside the shop.

Lauren breathed in the faint aroma of blackcurrants that always seemed to fill the shop. It made her feel safe and welcome. There was a tapping of tiny claws as Walter, Mrs Fontana's black and white terrier, trotted up to greet her. Lauren bent down to stroke his soft little ears. There was no sign of Mrs Fontana, so she headed further into the shop, peering round several bookshelves to look for her. She found the elderly lady standing on a little stool, putting cookery books on to a shelf.

'Hello, Mrs Fontana,' she called.

'Oh! Lauren,' said Mrs Fontana. She stepped down from the stool at once. 'I'm pleased that you've dropped by. I had a feeling that you would. I have something very important to give –'

'Actually, I've come about my friend Mel's pony, Shadow,' Lauren blurted out, not waiting for Mrs Fontana to finish. 'He's very sick.'

She stopped as Mrs Fontana held up one hand. 'I already know,' she said, pulling her soft yellow shawl around her shoulders. 'That's exactly what I wanted to talk to you about.'

Lauren tried not to let her mouth drop open. She knew Mrs Fontana quite well by now, but it was still a surprise when she knew things before Lauren had mentioned them.

'Poor Shadow is in a very bad way,'

Mrs Fontana went on. 'But there might be a way you can help him. Follow me, my dear.'

She walked to the back of the shop with Walter at her heels. Lauren followed, her mind buzzing with questions.

'I don't understand why Twilight couldn't heal him,' she said, as Mrs Fontana reached a green beaded curtain hanging in a doorway. 'We went to Goose Creek Farm last night and Twilight touched him with his horn. But nothing happened – Shadow just lay there and now he's even worse. Has something happened to Twilight's magical powers? We haven't been wasting them, I promise, and I've been trying my best to be a good Unicorn Friend . . .'

Mrs Fontana nodded. 'You don't need to worry about that,' she said. 'You've been a wonderful Unicorn Friend to Twilight, and you haven't been wasting his powers.'

She led Lauren through the curtain and into a cosy living room, with a big green sofa and two comfy-looking armchairs. There was also a marble fireplace with a big mantelpiece, and above it hung a beautiful painting of a unicorn drinking from a mountain stream. Lauren stared at it, enchanted. The unicorn's coat looked so glossy that she wanted to reach out and stroke it.

'Now, sit down for a moment,' said Mrs Fontana, indicating the sofa. 'There's something I need to explain.'

Lauren sank on to the squashy sofa

and picked up a cushion to hug, hoping that Mrs Fontana wasn't about to give her bad news. Mrs Fontana sat down next to her and adjusted her shawl.

'Now,' she said, reaching over and taking one of Lauren's hands. 'You need to understand that Shadow's illness is not your fault, or Twilight's. Twilight's magic is getting stronger all the time, but there are some things that even he can't cure.'

Lauren's heart pounded. She'd thought Twilight's magic could cure anything! He'd even mended her friend Jo-Ann's broken leg when she fell off her pony in the woods. Lauren thought of Shadow lying in the straw, struggling to breathe

. . . and there was nothing they could do about it! 'Does that mean Shadow will just get sicker and sicker?' she said, her voice trembling.

'Well, he will if we don't do anything to help him,' Mrs Fontana said gently. 'But there is a more powerful kind of magic that might just work.'

She got up and went over to the big, marble mantelpiece. She reached up towards the painting and pushed it gently to one side. Lauren could see a little cubby hole in the wall behind it.

'This is what we need,' said Mrs Fontana as she opened the door to the cubby hole and pulled out a rolled-up sheet of parchment paper, tied with a little red ribbon. She moved the painting back into place, then walked across the room and handed the scroll to Lauren. 'You can open it later.'

'What is it?' Lauren asked, fingering the rough paper curiously. It felt very old.

'It's a map,' Mrs Fontana explained. 'It will show you how to reach a place called the Plateau of Light up in the Blue Ridge Mountains.'

'The Blue Ridge Mountains?' Lauren frowned. The mountains were not far from her home – in fact she could see them quite clearly from Granger's Farm. But she'd never been there, certainly not on her own. And she had never heard of the Plateau of Light.

Mrs Fontana smiled. 'It's not too far for Twilight to fly,' she assured Lauren. 'The plateau is a magical place that appears just once a year, on a full moon. On that night, the Unicorn Elders gather there to welcome the unicorns that are returning to Arcadia. You know that some unicorns are chosen to return home, don't you?'

Lauren nodded. She knew about this all too well because Twilight had been offered the chance to go back to Arcadia himself. Unicorns were chosen to return to Arcadia when they had shown themselves to be especially brave and helpful, and it was a great honour. But it meant that they could never return to

Earth. Sidra was the Unicorn Elder who had visited Twilight to tell him that he had been chosen to return to Arcadia. Lauren had met her when Twilight had asked to stay on Earth. Thankfully Sidra had agreed, and allowed Twilight to stay.

'Well,' Mrs Fontana went on, 'tonight is the night that the Elders are gathering. Their magic is the strongest of all unicorn magic. If anyone can make Shadow better, they can. You need to go and ask them for help.' She looked at Lauren kindly. 'It's a long way to go, especially in the dark. You must make sure that you have plenty of warm clothes, because it can get very cold in the mountains at night. But I'm sure that you and Twilight can manage it.'

Lauren stared down at the rolled-up map, her mind whirling. 'You mean, we actually have to go and meet the unicorns that are going back to Arcadia?'

'The returning unicorns will be at the plateau,' said Mrs Fontana. 'But it's the Elders that you need to talk to about Shadow.'

Lauren felt fear clutch her heart. Taking Twilight to the ceremony at the plateau seemed like a huge risk. What if he saw all the other unicorns going back to Arcadia, and decided to go with them? She might lose him after all . . . But she couldn't say that to Mrs Fontana.

'What if we get lost?' she asked instead.

'The map will show you which way to go,' Mrs Fontana replied. 'But you will have to make sure you arrive at the right time. The unicorns are only there for a little while before they set off for Arcadia. You need to get there by midnight.'

Lauren took a deep breath. All sorts of thoughts were going through her mind. She wanted to say that she couldn't possibly manage a journey like that in the middle of the night, especially as it might mean losing Twilight! But then she thought of Shadow lying in the straw, and she knew she couldn't let him and Mel down. 'Thank you, Mrs Fontana,' she said. 'We'll do our best.'

Mrs Fontana smiled. 'This will be the most difficult task for you and Twilight so far, but I'm sure that you will find your way. You're a brave girl, and that's one of the reasons why you're such a good Unicorn Friend. Twilight is very lucky to have you.'

CHAPTER

Four

Lauren was very quiet on the journey back home to Granger's Farm. Right now, she didn't feel like a brave Unicorn Friend. In fact, she felt more and more nervous about her trip to the mountains with Twilight. It would be scary going so far at night, and they might get lost however hard she studied the map. But deep down, she knew that she wasn't really worried about the journey. The truth was that she was terrified of what might happen if she took Twilight to the unicorns' meeting. What if he decided he wanted to go back to Arcadia after all, with all the other unicorns?

'Is everything all right, Lauren?' asked Mrs Foster, breaking into her thoughts.

'Oh – I'm just thinking about a few things,' Lauren said hastily.

'You can phone Mel as soon as we get home,' said Mrs Foster. 'Maybe Shadow will be feeling better by now.'

Lauren crossed her fingers, hoping desperately that it was true. Maybe the vet would have found out what was wrong and been able to treat Shadow after all. And then she wouldn't have to take Twilight to the Plateau of Light.

They picked up Max and Buddy from Steven and Leo's house. Buddy bounded into the car and covered Lauren's face in slobbery licks, which cheered her up for a few moments. Max was full of what had happened that day. Buddy had sniffed out an old bone buried in the garden, and he'd got covered in mud digging it up with Leo's puppy, Buggy. The boys had ended up giving both dogs a bath, but of course the dogs hadn't wanted to stay in the tub. They had jumped out and run downstairs, covered in soap bubbles!

Lauren listened and laughed, glad of something else to think about. But as soon as they were home, she went to the phone to call Mel.

It was Mel who answered the phone. 'Hi, Lauren,' she said in a flat voice.

'Is Shadow any better?' Lauren asked, but she guessed from Mel's voice what the answer would be.

'No,' said Mel. Her voice wobbled. 'I think he's worse. He hasn't moved all day. He just lies there in the straw and he's breathing so heavily . . .' She stopped, and Lauren could hear that she was crying. Lauren felt her own throat closing up.

'The blood-test results have come in

but it's still not clear what's wrong,' Mel went on, sniffing. 'The vet came back this afternoon. He says it must be some kind of respiratory virus, which means there is something wrong with his lungs, but he doesn't understand why Shadow is getting worse so quickly.'

'Oh, Mel, I'm so sorry,' said Lauren. 'I'll come over first thing tomorrow.' She wished she could tell Mel what she was planning, but that was impossible. 'Don't give up hope. Shadow's such a strong, brave pony. He'll fight as hard as he can to get better.'

'Thanks, Lauren,' sniffed Mel. 'I'd better go. I don't want to leave Shadow on his own for too long. Mum says I can spend the night with him in his stable.'

'OK. Bye, Mel,' said Lauren. She put the phone down, imagining Mel curled up sadly in the straw next to her dapple-grey pony. The thought made tears prick her eyes, and she knew there really was no choice. She and Twilight had to go to the Blue Ridge Mountains to speak to the Unicorn Elders.

Lauren went out to the paddock to tell Twilight what they were going to do. She couldn't change him into a unicorn while people were around – it was too risky. But she knew he would understand what she had to tell him.

She fetched some pony nuts from the feed store and climbed over the rail at the edge of the paddock. Twilight greeted her with a whinny, as he always did, and she fed him the handful of nuts. 'I've been to see Mrs Fontana,' she told him, stroking his soft muzzle. 'She says there's nothing wrong with your powers. It's just that Shadow is too sick for you to cure him.'

Twilight stopped chewing the pony nuts, and his head drooped a little.

'But it's not our fault,' Lauren added hastily. 'Mrs Fontana says we might be able to help Shadow, but only if we make a special trip to the Blue Ridge Mountains to meet the Unicorn Elders.'

Twilight perked up again, his big brown eyes looking curious. Lauren hesitated, wondering whether to tell him about the unicorns going back to Arcadia, and the Plateau of Light.

'We have to get there by midnight,' she began. Then she stopped. She couldn't tell him why the unicorns were gathering. She just couldn't. She was too scared that he might want to join them.

'I'll come back out when everyone has gone to bed,' she whispered, and Twilight nuzzled her affectionately. Lauren knew he was trying to tell her that everything would be all right, and she felt bad for not telling him the full story. But she'd tell him later, when they could talk about it properly. She fetched him some hay and went back inside.

She went straight upstairs to her bedroom to look at the map. With trembling fingers, she undid the scrap of red ribbon and let the parchment unfurl. The map was drawn in spidery silver ink that glimmered in the fading light from her bedroom window. Lauren pored over it, tracing her finger over the mountains and valleys criss-crossed with winding rivers. The Plateau of Light was marked with a glowing, golden square halfway up one of the tallest mountain peaks. It looked like such a long way. She took a deep breath and looked out of the window at Twilight. He looked up at her from the paddock and whinnied. He was obviously waiting for their adventure to begin.

Lauren's heart did a little somersault.

Please, please, Twilight, don't ever leave me. Please don't go back to Arcadia.

Her dad called her down to dinner, so Lauren put the map to one side and went downstairs. There were sausages and green beans to go with the baked potatoes, and Mr Foster began to serve it up.

'Feeling hungry, Lauren?' he asked, as he held up three sausages with the serving tongs.

Lauren smiled weakly. Usually, sausages and baked potatoes was one of her favourite dinners, but today there were butterflies fluttering around her stomach and she didn't feel like eating at all. 'Not very,' she admitted. 'Two will be plenty, thanks, Dad.'

Mr Foster raised his eyebrows in surprise. 'Well, that means all the more for the rest of us, doesn't it?' he commented cheerfully.

Mrs Foster flashed Lauren a sympathetic smile. 'I expect you're worried about Shadow, aren't you?'

Lauren nodded. 'Mel says he's getting worse,' she said. 'And the vet still doesn't know what's wrong with him. The blood tests didn't show anything.'

'Oh dear,' sighed her mum. 'We'll just have to hope that a good night's rest will do Shadow some good.'

Lauren picked up her fork and played with her green beans, but she could only manage a few mouthfuls. She kept thinking about the journey ahead, and the moment when she would have to tell Twilight the truth about the Plateau of Light. The more she thought about it, the more nervous she felt, and she just wished it was time to go and get it over with. It was a relief when dinner was over and she could finally leave the table.

'I think I'll have an early night,' she said, heading for the stairs. 'I'm going to get up early tomorrow to go and see Mel.'

'That's fine, honey,' said her mum. 'Try not to worry. Shadow might be a lot better by then.'

⋆

In her bedroom, Lauren had another quick look at the map. She wondered what it would be like in the mountains at night. Mrs Fontana had said it would be cold, so she would have to be prepared. She'd need warm clothes, an apple for Twilight and some water, but she couldn't do anything until everyone else had come upstairs. So she lay down on her bed and stared up at the ceiling, listening to what was happening in the rest of the house. She heard Max going to bed, then she heard the faint sound of the TV in the living room. She guessed that her mum and dad were watching a film. The minutes ticked by very slowly.

At last, Mr and Mrs Foster climbed the stairs and Lauren heard the click of their bedroom door closing shut. She got up and took her warmest jacket out of her wardrobe and rummaged for her rucksack in her cupboard. She shrugged on the jacket and put the map into one of the zip-up pockets. She packed a little blanket, just in case it got really cold, and then crept out of her room and down the stairs. As quietly as she could, she stuffed a plastic bottle of water and an apple in with the blanket and slung the rucksack over her shoulders. Then she slipped out of the house. It was quite chilly already, but there was a full moon, so she could see quite clearly.

Twilight was waiting for her at the gate. 'It's time to go, Twilight,' she whispered. She muttered the words of the Turning Spell, and Twilight turned into a snowy white unicorn.

He shook his mane, making it sparkle in the moonlight. 'Thank you for trying to help Shadow,' he said. 'I can tell you're nervous about the journey to the mountains, but I promise I'll look after you.'

Lauren felt a stab of guilt. She still hadn't told Twilight about the ceremony for unicorns returning to Arcadia. She couldn't let him know she was more nervous about that than the journey.

She gave him a hug for good luck, then vaulted up on to his back and fished the map out of her pocket. 'OK, Twilight,' she said. 'There's a big craggy mountain that we have to head towards. I think we'll see it once we've flown over the woods. Fly as fast as you can!'

She gave him a little nudge with her heels. The unicorn snorted and tossed his head, then soared upward into the night.

CHAPTER Five

Twilight plunged forward, and Lauren buried her hands in his mane. He galloped into the starry sky faster than she'd ever known him go before, and the wind made her eyes water as they sped towards the Blue Ridge Mountains. They flew over the woods and then she started looking out for the big craggy mountain.

The full moon made the landscape below surprisingly bright, and Lauren peered down, trying to match the trees and winding rivers with the lines on the silvery map. There was the sweeping bend of a river, and a big, sprawling farm on its banks. Then, up ahead, she spotted the dark bulk of the mountain range and the craggy mountain that was marked on the map, and she realized in relief that they were going in the right direction.

Twilight flew confidently over the foothills and then through sweeping valleys with the mountains rising up on either side. Lauren gazed down at the hickory forests that covered them, and heard an owl hooting somewhere in their depths. Another owl replied, its call echoing eerily along the valley. Lauren kept her hands twisted in Twilight's mane, trying not to feel afraid.

As they drew closer to the mountains, the wind grew stronger, and Twilight sometimes had to struggle against it as he climbed steadily upward. Lauren huddled on his back, feeling glad she'd worn her warmest jacket. Tugged by the wind, the map flapped wildly in Lauren's fingers. Suddenly it was whipped free and snatched into the air.

'Oh no!' Lauren gasped. 'Twilight! I've lost the map!'

She peered down in dismay as the

piece of parchment fluttered towards the forest.

'Fly after it!' she cried desperately. 'Otherwise we'll never find our way to the mountain!'

Twilight swooped down after the fluttering paper, so steeply that Lauren was afraid she would slide over his head. She clung on to his neck as the map reached the forest and disappeared among the mass of branches and spring leaves.

'We *have* to find it!' Lauren exclaimed, and Twilight plunged in between the treetops, snapping twigs and sending branches springing back into Lauren's face. She ducked and covered her face with one hand to avoid being scratched. At last there was a gentle thud, and Twilight landed on the forest floor at the foot of a towering oak tree. It was much darker down here because the branches kept out the moonlight.

Lauren looked around, trying to see what had happened to the precious parchment. 'Can you see it, Twilight?' she whispered.

'Not yet,' replied the unicorn. 'But we'll find it, I know we will.' He wove in and out of the towering tree trunks while Lauren peered into the darkness. How could she have let the map go? She should have gripped it more tightly . . .

A little stream glimmered up ahead and Lauren's heart gave a leap. She could just see the map, one edge poking up among some reeds. 'There it is!' she cried.

Twilight broke into a canter. When they reached the stream, Lauren scrambled down from his back and stretched out with one hand to pick up the map. It had landed face down among the reeds, and the bottom half had dipped right into the water.

'It's all wet,' she said anxiously. She smoothed the map out with her fingers and looked at it closely. She could just see some of the silvery lines, but at least half of them had been washed away. 'I can't read it any more! How will we find the way now?' She felt like bursting into tears. 'I can't believe I dropped it – it was really stupid of me!'

'It wasn't your fault,' said Twilight. He blew gently into her hair. 'It was the wind. And you're not stupid at all – you're trying to save Shadow. I know you can do it. I trust you, Lauren.'

Lauren looked up at him. 'Do you really?' she asked.

Twilight snorted, and nudged her arm. 'I trust you more than anyone else in the world, Lauren. Now, we have to work out where we're going. How much of the map do you think you can remember?'

Lauren let go of Twilight and looked down at the map again. She concentrated hard, trying to picture the bits that had been washed away. It was difficult, but when she looked more closely, there were just enough silvery lines left to jog her memory. 'I think I can remember enough,' she said. 'We'd better go. It must be nearly midnight!'

She vaulted on to Twilight's back and he took off, making his way swiftly up between the trees. As they cleared them, Lauren directed him once more towards the craggy mountain. As they drew closer, she could see a deep cleft in the mountainside and knew that this was what they must aim for. She remembered the way it had been drawn in silver on the map.

'That way!' she cried, and Twilight changed course, flying strongly against the buffeting wind. Lauren sat tight, screwing up her eyes against the icy gusts. But inside, she felt much warmer. *I trust you more than anyone else in the world, Lauren* – that was what Twilight had said. Maybe if he trusted her so much, she should trust him too. Enough to believe that he wouldn't change his mind about staying with her if he found out about the Plateau of Light . . .

'We're almost at the top of the mountain,' said Twilight, as he swooped up towards the highest peak, where little patches of snow lay on the ground. He puffed as he struggled to fly against a powerful gust of wind. 'I don't think I can fly all the way up. What if you get blown off? Can we land somewhere and walk the rest of the way?'

Lauren looked around. There were no more trees, and she knew the plateau must be very near. 'Maybe you're right,' she agreed. 'You can land here, Twilight.'

Twilight came to a stop on a big flat rock and waited for Lauren to get down.

'Now what happens?' asked Twilight,

looking at Lauren with his trusting brown eyes. 'Where are we meeting the Elders?'

Lauren took a deep breath. She knew that the moment had come for her to tell Twilight the whole truth. 'We're . . . we're going to the Plateau of Light,' she told him. 'It's the place where all the chosen unicorns go before –'

'The Plateau of Light?' Twilight echoed, his eyes stretched wide. 'Sidra told me all about it; how all the unicorns who are going back to Arcadia gather there once a year.'

Lauren felt a little stab of anxiety. Twilight knew about it already! And he seemed really excited about the ceremony. Did that mean he wanted to go back to Arcadia with the other unicorns? Suddenly, she didn't want him to come to the plateau with her, in case he decided to leave her after all. 'Well,' she said. 'I have to go and speak to the Elders, but maybe you should wait here . . .'

Twilight swished his tail. 'But I want to come!' he insisted. He looked up at the steep, rocky mountainside. 'And anyway, you can't go up there on your own. It's too dangerous.'

Lauren swallowed, trying to remember what she'd been thinking about trust. It felt awful, not knowing for sure if Twilight would want to stay with her once he had seen the ceremony. She turned away, feeling tears prick her eyes.

Quiet hoofbeats followed her, and a moment later she felt Twilight snuffle her hair, his breath warm on her neck. 'What's wrong, Lauren?' he asked.

Lauren swallowed hard. 'I didn't want to tell you we were coming to the Plateau of Light because I was afraid you would change your mind about staying with me,' she said all in a rush. 'I thought you'd see the other unicorns, and the Unicorn Elders, and want to go back to Arcadia with them.'

She turned round to see Twilight looking at her in astonishment. 'Of course I won't!' He lowered his head and nuzzled her hands. 'I'm sorry you were so worried about it. But you can trust me, I promise. I came here with you because I believe we can help Shadow. I love having adventures with you! I just want to see the ceremony, that's all.'

Lauren threw her arms around his neck and gave him a big hug, until his mane tickled her nose and she had to step back before she sneezed. 'I love having adventures with you, too,' she said. 'And you're right, we need to concentrate on helping Shadow!' She fished in her rucksack for the apple and fed it to Twilight, then shared the bottle of water with him, pouring some into her cupped hand so that he could drink it.

'OK, Twilight,' she said, when they had finished their snack. She rested her hand on his mane. 'Let's go to the Plateau of Light.'

CHAPTER Six

Lauren and Twilight began to struggle up the steep slope against the biting wind. Lauren kept her fingers twisted in the unicorn's mane, just in case she slipped on the icy rocks. Sometimes they dislodged stones with their feet, sending them clattering down the mountainside. They seemed to fall a long, long way. Lauren was very glad

Twilight was beside her. It would have been very scary, scrambling up here on her own.

'Not . . . far . . . now,' she muttered between gritted teeth. She concentrated on placing one foot in front of the other, sometimes bending down to use her free hand to haul herself up.

At last they reached the top of the mountain, and Lauren leaned her shoulder against Twilight's to get her breath back. Then, side by side, they peered over the peak. Miraculously, the wind dropped, and Lauren gasped out loud.

The whole of the plateau was bathed in gentle, golden light, which came from a wide circle of glowing rocks. In the centre of the circle stood three lines of unicorns, their white coats gleaming and their horns shimmering. They were all standing with their heads bowed, facing a rock that glowed more brightly than the others. The unicorns seemed to be waiting for something, and the air fizzed with magic and expectation.

As she looked more closely, Lauren realized that there were three more unicorns, taller than the others, standing right in front of the great rock. They stepped further into the circle, out of the dazzling light, and Lauren saw them more clearly. One of them had a bronze horn, one had a golden horn, and the third had a glimmering silver horn.

Lauren recognized the silver-horned unicorn at once.

'It's Sidra!' she breathed, and Twilight nodded.

Lauren placed her hand on Twilight's neck and together they ducked down behind a boulder. It felt strange for her to be spying on the special unicorn ceremony, even though she knew that Mrs Fontana had sent her here. After a couple of moments she heard Sidra's voice ringing out clearly.

'It is time for the ceremony to begin,' she announced. 'Ira, Rohan, let us take our places. Our chosen ones must begin their journey to Arcadia.'

Twilight whispered to Lauren that Ira and Rohan were the other two Unicorn Elders, with the gold and bronze horns. Lauren was growing more and more curious to see what was going on.

Standing on tiptoe, she peered over the rock.

One by one, the chosen unicorns walked up to the great rock. They bent their heads to be touched in turn by the gold, silver and bronze horns of the Elders. The Elders' horns glowed as they touched the earthly unicorns, confirming that their lives were about to change forever as they returned to Arcadia.

'Well done,' Sidra said to each one. 'You have shown yourself to be a wise and giving unicorn. We are proud to take you back to Arcadia with us.'

Lauren couldn't help noticing that each earthly unicorn raised its head proudly when Sidra spoke to them.

Returning to Arcadia was making them so happy! She felt her heart twist at the thought that Twilight could have gone through this ceremony too – but she'd encouraged him to stay on earth. Had it been the right thing to do? Was he really as happy living with her as he would be in Arcadia with all the other unicorns?

She glanced at him. His ears were pricked up and his eyes were shining, but when he felt Lauren looking at him, he turned and rested his head reassuringly on her shoulder. Lauren reached up to stroke his nose. She had promised to trust him, which meant she had to believe that he truly wanted to stay with her.

The ceremony was coming to an end. Lauren watched as the last of the unicorns received their welcome from the Elders and trotted to join the others, whinnying happily.

Then Sidra addressed them all. 'Arcadia is waiting for you. You will now join your brothers and sisters, who, like you, have all gained wisdom from their important lessons on Earth.'

The unicorns listened intently. Then the unicorn with the golden horn stepped forward, his snowy coat rippling under the light of the glowing rocks. 'I am Rohan. I will lead you to Arcadia,' he announced. 'Say your farewells to this Earth. You will never return, and I know many of you must be feeling sad to have left your loyal Unicorn Friends behind.'

There was a murmur of agreement from the gathered unicorns, and Rohan bowed his head, as though he was acknowledging that even this exciting moment had a sad side. 'But always remember this,' he went on after a while. 'Your Unicorn Friends are still there. They have not ceased to be your friends just because you have parted from them. You will be able to watch over them from Arcadia, and make sure that they are safe.'

He looked round at Ira, who stepped forward and gave a piercing whinny. 'And now, dear unicorns, it is time for us to go!'

There was a ripple of excitement among the unicorns. Many of them appeared to take one last look at the mountains. Then Rohan reared up, his hooves flashing in the night air. 'Follow me!' he cried, and leapt into the starry sky.

Ira joined him, and one by one the chosen unicorns took off from the plateau. For a few moments, Rohan hovered in one place as the unicorns circled around him like a flock of graceful snow-coloured birds.

Lauren's heart was pounding. Sidra hadn't taken off yet. She had to speak to her, but Lauren was terrified that the Unicorn Elder would be angry with her for watching the ceremony.

But then she thought of Shadow, lying in his stable, struggling to breathe. He needed their help! And that meant they had done the right thing by coming here. She just had to show herself before it was too late –

A voice interrupted her thoughts.

'Lauren! Twilight!' Sidra called. 'I know you are there. Come out from your hiding place. I must speak to you!'

CHAPTER

Seven

Lauren felt her legs tremble with panic. Sidra had known they were there all along! Would she refuse to help them because they had watched the ceremony? Slowly, clinging on to Twilight's mane, she peeped round the boulder. Sidra was standing just in front of it – but to Lauren's relief, her brown eyes looked soft and welcoming.

'Don't be afraid, Lauren,' said Sidra.

'How . . . how did you know we were here?' Lauren stuttered.

The Elder chuckled. 'Unicorn Elders

know all sorts of things,' she said. 'I am very happy to see you both. Watching the ceremony is a great honour, but you are worthy of it. Believe me, we would have stopped you if we thought you weren't.' She stretched her neck towards Twilight, who stepped forward eagerly to greet her.

'We didn't come to spy,' Lauren promised. 'We've come to ask if you can help Twilight's friend Shadow. He's really sick and Mrs Fontana told me that you were his only hope.'

Sidra nodded. 'Yes, I know,' she said, her voice becoming grave. 'Shadow is in great danger, and you were right to come here. We must hurry because soon it will be too late to do anything to help him.'

Lauren glanced at the unicorns above her, hovering in the air while they waited for Sidra.

'But . . . but . . . we're not going to Arcadia, are we?' she stammered, her mouth going dry. 'Can't you just give me something to cure Shadow?'

The Unicorn Elder reached forward and blew gently into Lauren's hair. 'No, my dear,' she said. 'You must come with me, and Twilight must come too.'

Lauren leaned against Twilight's shoulder, doubts flooding through her. They had already travelled so far, and now they were heading to Arcadia itself!

What if they couldn't get back once they'd got there? Or what if Twilight decided to stay?

'Don't worry, Lauren,' Twilight whispered. 'We must do this for Shadow. Remember how badly he needs us. I'll make sure we get back safely.' He turned his head towards Sidra. 'I am ready to come with you.'

'What about you, Lauren?' Sidra asked. 'Are you ready to come to Arcadia?'

Lauren met the Unicorn Elder's gaze, and felt Twilight's warm, strong shoulder against hers. Twilight was right – they had come all this way for Shadow and they couldn't let him down now. She took a deep breath and pushed all her doubts to one side. 'Yes, I'm ready,' she said bravely.

Sidra's eyes glowed. Then she turned on her haunches, galloped across the plateau and took off from the centre of the circle. Her hooves left a trail of silvery sparks as she rose into the sky to join the waiting unicorns.

Lauren scrambled on to Twilight's back and he set off after the Unicorn Elder, his hooves ringing on the rocks as he entered the glowing circle. Then he too lifted into the air and soared upward. Lauren glanced down and felt dizzy. They were so high up that even the top of the mountain looked a long way down. But strangely, she had stopped feeling cold, and the wind seemed to have lost its icy bite.

Sidra circled around them and then swooped in close. 'We are going to follow the others to the edge of Arcadia,' she said. 'Shadow needs water from the Waterfall of Stars, which is the source of all unicorn magic.'

'Is the waterfall *inside* Arcadia?' asked Lauren. She realized that she would love to see the wonderful place that she had read and heard so much about, but she was still feeling a little bit nervous.

'No,' said Sidra. 'The Waterfall of Stars falls from the sky and enters our magical land as a giant cascade of water and light. It lies just outside the boundary of Arcadia.'

'How amazing,' Lauren breathed. Seeing the Plateau of Light was wonderful enough, but the Waterfall of Stars sounded even more incredible!

Sidra tossed her mane and touched Twilight's neck with her horn, which glowed even more brightly than before. 'I'm giving you some of my energy,' she told him. 'You will need it, especially as you've already flown a long way tonight. We're going to fly quickly, so we reach Arcadia before morning. Stay close behind me, Twilight.'

She turned away and galloped towards

the flock of unicorns. Lauren buried her hands in Twilight's mane as he raced after the Unicorn Elder. When Rohan and Ira saw them coming, they whinnied loudly and plunged forward, a stream of silvery hoofprints lingering in the air behind them as they led the unicorns into the starry night.

CHAPTER

Eight

Lauren felt a thrill of excitement as Twilight caught up with the other unicorns. There was a beautiful young unicorn to their right, who turned her head as Twilight drew alongside. Her coat wasn't pure white like the others, but had the faintest peachy tinge, like the sky just before dawn.

'Welcome, Lauren and Twilight,' she

whinnied, a little breathlessly. 'My name is Frost. You are both very brave to have come on this long journey.'

Twilight reached out his nose towards her. 'We just want our friend Shadow to get better,' he said.

Frost nodded, and blinked her long eyelashes. 'Yes. But not everyone would be brave enough to come all the way to the Plateau of Light.'

Lauren wondered who had been Frost's Unicorn Friend, and whether it had been a sad parting. It must have been – she could hardly bear to imagine how it must have felt for the unicorn or the child left behind. She gripped Twilight a little bit tighter with her knees, feeling very glad that he had promised to stay with her.

Frost looked up at Lauren. 'I can guess what you're thinking, Lauren. You are right that it was hard to part with my Unicorn Friend. But it was the right time for me to leave – we both knew that. I wouldn't have agreed to return to Arcadia if he hadn't been ready for it. And I know I'll always be able to watch over him.'

Lauren hugged Twilight's neck. It was good to hear that Frost hadn't left her Unicorn Friend against his will. Maybe the Elders never allowed that to happen. She hoped so – she really hoped so . . .

The unicorns swept on and on into the night. Lauren was beginning to feel exhausted. Her fingers felt almost frozen to Twilight's mane, and her back ached from riding for so long. They were so high up that it was difficult to tell what lay below. Every now and again they galloped through a drift of fluffy clouds, and she felt refreshed by their soft, moist touch, like the softest cotton wool.

Then, just as her eyelids began to droop, she saw something twinkling up ahead. She craned her neck, trying to work out what it was. When they drew closer, she gasped. It was as though a thousand diamonds were tumbling through the sky, their light reflecting in all directions. It was the most incredible thing Lauren had ever seen, like something out of a beautiful dream. It must be the Waterfall of Stars!

She looked down. The sky was growing lighter, and she could see through swirls of mist and cloud to the land below. There were lush green meadows dotted with trees and wild flowers and sparkling, crystal-clear streams. Lauren felt puzzled because she could see quite clearly, but the sun still hadn't appeared over the horizon. Then she realized that not one but two moons shone above them, casting a soft glow over the landscape.

Sidra circled the clouds and came back alongside Twilight. 'We are flying over Arcadia,' she explained. 'But we will not stop here. The others are about to descend, but we will carry on without them. You can see the Waterfall of Stars ahead, which is where we must go.'

Rohan and Ira were beginning to canter in wide circles, getting gradually lower and lower. The other unicorns followed, their manes and tails streaming behind them as they swooped after the Elders.

'Goodbye, Lauren and Twilight,' Frost called as she passed them.

'Goodbye,' cried Lauren. Twilight tossed his mane and whinnied.

Sidra and Twilight hovered in one place until all the other unicorns had gone past. As well as the twin Arcadian moons, the light from the Waterfall of Stars was very bright, reflecting flashes of light from the unicorns' hooves as they galloped through the air. Twilight gazed after them with his ears pricked up. Lauren reached down and stroked his neck. She hoped he wasn't feeling too disappointed at being left behind.

As the unicorns became small white specks below, Sidra turned to them. 'It's not far now,' she said. 'When we get nearer, Twilight, stay close beside me.' And with a swish of her moon-coloured tail, she set off at a gallop once more.

On they flew, until the waterfall seemed to stretch out to fill the whole sky ahead of them. Up close, it was so dazzling that Lauren had to screw up her eyes to look at it. She felt very small next to the shimmering curtain of stars, but at the same time the light filled her with happiness, as though she'd just opened all the birthday and Christmas presents she'd ever wanted.

Soon, the waterfall was towering above

them, and Lauren could see that the thundering cascade was made of pure, sparkling water mingled with millions of tiny stars. Water and stars tumbled down into a pool far below. Lauren felt fine, cool spray on her cheeks and eyelashes, and saw tiny droplets settle in Twilight's mane.

'You need to take some of the water back to Shadow,' instructed Sidra.

For a second, Lauren panicked. How were they going to do that? She hadn't realized she needed to bring an empty container!

Twilight turned his head to look at her. 'What about your water bottle?' he suggested. 'We could carry some water in that.'

'That's a great idea!' she said. She pulled the plastic bottle out of her rucksack and unscrewed the top. She poured out what was left of the regular water and gave it a shake to make sure the last drops fell out.

'Do I just lean into the waterfall to fill it up?' she called to Sidra. The noise of the water was pounding in her ears, and the pool of splashing starlight seemed a long, long way below. Lauren gulped as she imagined being swept off Twilight's back by the force of the water, down, down, down . . .

Sidra nodded. 'You'll need to get closer,' she warned.

Lauren told herself that the Unicorn

Elder wouldn't ask her to do something that was dangerous. But it still felt very scary as Twilight cantered towards the roaring, sparkling water. Lauren held the plastic bottle firmly and stretched it out towards the waterfall. But she couldn't reach the water even when she leaned over as far as she dared.

'We'll have to get even closer, Twilight!' she called, clinging on to his mane.

Sidra drew alongside Twilight, so close that she was almost touching him, and the air between them seemed to crackle with magic. Sidra's horn glowed, and Lauren knew that she was giving Twilight some of her strength.

'Now try!' said Sidra.

With a huge effort, Twilight cantered one stride closer to the curtain of rushing water and Lauren took her chance. Gripping tightly with her knees, she stretched out and plunged her hand into the water.

She expected the water to be freezing, but instead it felt fresh and clear and comforting and warm all at the same time, like ice-cold lemonade on a hot day or a mug of hot chocolate on a cold one. Lauren laughed out loud. It was wonderful! She brought out her hand and saw that the water bottle was full, so she screwed the top back on and stowed it carefully in her jacket pocket.

'I've got it!' she cried breathlessly.

'Well done!' Sidra called. 'Now we must go!'

The two unicorns backed away from the tower of water and stars. Being so close to the waterfall seemed to have given Twilight even more energy. He bounded after Sidra and they sped through the sky, back towards the Plateau of Light. Lauren's fingers were still tingling with the lovely feeling from the sparkling water, and when she looked down she could see the faintest sheen on her skin, like a dusting of diamonds.

They passed over Arcadia once more, and Lauren gazed down at it, wondering how Frost and the other new arrivals were settling in.

'I would love to show you Arcadia,' said Sidra. 'One day, perhaps, you will be able to visit. But now is not the time. Shadow needs you. You must take the water to him as quickly as you can.'

The journey to the plateau seemed to speed past, and Lauren soon saw the mountains looming ahead. Sidra circled the peak and landed gently in the ring of rocks, her hooves pounding against the stone.

'You have both done well,' she told them, her brown eyes shining. She touched Twilight with her silvery horn, and it glowed strongly once more. 'Twilight, you have shown yourself to be strong and tireless as well as brave. I give you now the energy you will need to reach Shadow in time.'

'Thank you, Sidra,' said Twilight, his ears pricked up.

Sidra looked at Lauren. 'Farewell, Lauren. I'm sure we will meet again, but meanwhile, continue to be a good friend to Twilight. I know you will always do your best.'

Lauren nodded. 'Goodbye, Sidra,' she said breathlessly. 'And thank you. It was amazing to see the waterfall.'

Sidra arched her neck and gave a trumpeting whinny that carried over the mountains. Then she rose into the air and flew off, back towards Arcadia.

Lauren patted Twilight's neck as they watched her disappear into the indigo sky. 'That was the most amazing adventure ever!' she whispered. Then she took the bottle out of her pocket and gazed at the starry water that sparkled inside. 'Come on. We'd better get back to Shadow.'

CHAPTER Nine

Twilight shook his silky mane and took off again. Lauren stroked his neck and did her best to encourage him – even with Sidra's help, she knew he must be exhausted by now. Her eyelids were beginning to feel very heavy and she had to concentrate hard on staying awake.

'Are you feeling all right?' she asked

Twilight, as they cantered above the forest that stretched over the lower slopes of the mountains. 'I'm almost falling asleep.'

'I'm fine,' said Twilight. 'But I'd be worn out if Sidra hadn't given me that extra boost of strength.' All the same, he did sound a little bit tired, and Lauren wondered if he was feeling sad too, now that they'd left Arcadia behind.

Lauren forced herself to ask a difficult question. 'Was it hard, seeing all the other unicorns going back to Arcadia?'

Twilight twitched one ear. 'Not really,' he said. 'It was lovely to have a look at Arcadia but I know we didn't have time for a proper visit. Anyway, seeing the waterfall was exciting enough.'

'Are you sure?' Lauren said. 'You really didn't want to stay in Arcadia with Frost and the other unicorns?'

Twilight shook his mane vigorously. 'Lauren, I've told you. I really want to stay with you!'

'Oh . . .' Lauren breathed out happily. 'Thank you, Twilight.'

As they cantered onward, Lauren recognized the winding river that they'd flown over on the way to the mountains, and the big farm nestled on its banks. 'We'll be there soon,' she promised Twilight.

There was a faint glow over the horizon to the east. It was almost dawn. They had been out for the whole night! They began to soar down towards Goose Creek Farm, and Lauren felt for the precious bottle of water in her jacket pocket. It had to make Shadow better – it *had* to.

The yard was deserted, and Twilight landed right beside Shadow's stable. Lauren slid off his back and peered over the door. Shadow was still lying down, and Lauren could see his sides heaving painfully. His breathing sounded harsh and noisy, as if he had a sore throat. Mel was fast asleep beside him, wrapped up in a striped, woollen horse rug.

Very, very quietly, Lauren slid back the bolt and led Twilight inside. She knelt down beside Shadow's head and stroked his face. It felt damp with sweat, and he only half-opened his eyes at her touch. Lauren's heart lurched. He was even sicker than before – had they arrived in time?

'We've come to give you something to make you better,' she whispered, pulling the water bottle from her jacket pocket and unscrewing the lid. She lifted Shadow's head on to her lap and gently opened the corner of his mouth. She trickled some of the starry water in, and watched his throat to check that he had swallowed. A few droplets escaped and stayed on his velvety muzzle like tiny, quivering diamonds. Once Shadow had swallowed, Lauren trickled in a little bit more.

Shadow gave a huge sigh, as if drinking two mouthfuls had worn him out. Lauren gently laid his head back on the straw. Then she sat back and waited anxiously. A couple of minutes ticked past, and Shadow still didn't move.

'I've given him half the water,' Lauren whispered, looking up at Twilight. 'Do you think that's enough?'

Twilight nuzzled her shoulder. 'Wait a little bit longer,' he said. 'Look. His breathing's getting quieter.'

Lauren listened. 'Yes,' she said. 'And his sides aren't heaving up and down quite so much.'

As she spoke, Shadow's eyes flickered open and he gave a soft whicker. Then he closed his eyes again.

Twilight whickered back gently and turned to Lauren. 'I think he's going to be all right.'

Lauren leaned forward and arranged Shadow's forelock neatly. His skin already felt cooler, as if his fever had gone away. He was asleep now, and he looked peaceful and relaxed. She got to her feet and hugged Twilight.

'We did it!' she whispered.

Just then, Mel stirred and murmured something in her sleep. Lauren cast a final glance down at the sleeping pony. 'We'd better go before Mel wakes up.'

They crept out of the stable. Lauren climbed on to Twilight's back and he cantered into the air, keeping to the grass at the edge of the yard for the first few strides so that his hooves didn't make a noise on the concrete.

Lauren realized she was still gripping the half-empty bottle of starry water. 'What do you think I should do with the rest of the water, Twilight?' she asked. 'I don't think I should keep it, do you?'

'No,' Twilight agreed. 'It's much too magical. But we shouldn't just throw it away, either – that would be a waste.'

'It's a pity we don't have our own Waterfall of Stars,' Lauren said wistfully. 'Then we'd be able to fill a bottle whenever we needed it.'

Twilight arched his neck and whinnied. 'But maybe we could make one!' he exclaimed. 'We could pour the water into the creek that runs through the woods. It wouldn't make it as powerful as the real waterfall but it might give it a little bit of magic.'

Lauren beamed. 'That's a great idea! Maybe it will protect any animals that drink from it and stop them from getting sick.'

Twilight flew over the woods and landed by the creek, where the water bubbled over some rocks. The first pale yellow rays of sun were just beginning to filter through the trees, and as Lauren poured the starry water out of the bottle, it seemed as though the whole creek danced with light.

As they watched the pretty sparkling water, a young deer appeared on the other side of the creek. It walked slowly to the edge of the bank, looking tired and thirsty, and bent its head to drink. After a few sips, it glanced up, its eyes shining. With a twitch of its ears, it bounded back into the woods, seeming full of energy once more.

'I think it's working already,' Lauren murmured happily. She leaned against Twilight's shoulder, then wearily clambered on to his back for the last time. She yawned and rubbed her eyes. 'Time for us to go home.'

To Lauren's relief, the house was quiet when she crept inside, leaving Twilight in his paddock with a bucket of pony nuts. Even Buddy was still asleep, curled up in his basket beside the range. She tiptoed up to her bedroom, took off her jacket and peeled off her jeans and sweater, then crawled under her soft, comfy duvet. Within seconds, she was fast asleep.

'Lauren!'

Lauren was dreaming of a beautiful land far away, where herds of unicorns grazed among meadows full of red and yellow wild flowers. But there was a voice pulling her back . . .

'Lauren! You've overslept!'

Lauren opened her eyes and saw her mum smiling down at her.

'Hello, sleepyhead! I thought you were planning on getting up early,' said Mrs Foster. 'Weren't you going to Mel's first thing?'

Lauren sat bolt upright. How could

she have forgotten? She threw off her duvet and jumped up. 'Sorry, Mum,' she said. 'I . . . I don't know what happened . . .'

'Don't worry,' said Mrs Foster, heading back out of Lauren's room. 'You must have been very tired last night. But Mel phoned, so I said you'd call her back when you were awake.'

Lauren reached for her jeans and tugged them on. She glanced at her bedside clock. It was half past nine, so she'd only had a few hours' sleep. But to her surprise, she didn't feel tired at all. In fact, she felt full of energy! She quickly finished dressing, then dashed downstairs and phoned her friend.

Her heart was hammering as she dialled the number for Goose Creek Farm. Hopefully Shadow would be much, much better – but she couldn't be totally sure, not yet.

'Lauren!' Mel answered the phone. She sounded excited and happy, and Lauren felt relief sweep over her. 'You've got to come over right away! Shadow's loads better. When I woke up this morning, he was standing up and eating his hay!'

Half an hour later, Lauren and Twilight were trotting along the lane that led to Goose Creek Farm. Now that he was a shaggy grey pony again, Lauren couldn't ask Twilight how he was feeling, but she was pleased to see that he didn't seem too tired either. Maybe their visit to the Waterfall of Stars had done them both good, as well as Shadow.

As they trotted into the yard, Mel's face appeared over Shadow's door. She was smiling from ear to ear. 'Hi, Lauren!' she called. 'Thanks so much for riding over. Come and see Shadow. He's a *million* times better!'

Lauren dismounted and led Twilight across the yard, feeling butterflies of happiness tumbling around in her tummy. Sure enough, Shadow was standing by his haynet, looking as though there had never been anything wrong with him at all. When he saw Lauren and Twilight, he stopped eating and greeted them with a deep whicker, as if he knew exactly what they had done for him.

Mel let herself into the stable while Lauren tied Twilight outside, then Lauren followed her friend inside. Mel stroked Shadow's neck, then hugged him. 'The vet has been back,' she said. 'He looked really puzzled when he saw how much better Shadow was. He thinks Shadow must have fought off the virus on his own.'

'That's fantastic,' said Lauren. 'I'm so glad, Mel.'

She wished she could tell her friend about the unicorn ceremony at the Plateau of Light, or their amazing journey to fetch the bottle of starry water. She knew Mel would find it all so exciting! But it didn't really matter. The most important thing was that Shadow was better. And what was more, Lauren knew she could trust Twilight more deeply than she'd ever trusted him before – he had seen the beautiful land of Arcadia and he'd *still* chosen to stay with her!

Mel and Lauren watched as Twilight stuck his head over the half-door. The two ponies touched noses. Shadow's brown eyes shone as he whinnied softly, and Lauren guessed he was thanking Twilight for helping him. She felt a glow of pride light her up from inside. Twilight was so brave, and loyal, and clever. She was the luckiest Unicorn Friend in the whole world!

My Secret Unicorn

When Lauren recites a secret spell, Twilight turns into a beautiful unicorn with magical powers! Together Lauren and Twilight learn how to use their magic to help their friends.

Look out for more My Secret Unicorn adventures:

The Magic Spell,
Dreams Come True, Flying High,
Starlight Surprise, Stronger Than Magic,
A Special Friend, A Winter Wish, A Touch of Magic,
Snowy Dreams, Twilight Magic, Friends Forever, Rising Star,
Moonlight Journey, Keeper of Magic